MOSHI MOSHI

Jonathan London

illustrated by Yoshi Miyake

The Millbrook Press   Brookfield, Connecticut

For Tanzo Ishihara, and
Kenji Sato, Pen Pal—J. L.

To my daughter, Rosamond,
and my dear uncle and aunt,
A. & Y. Terayama, who helped
me with research—Y. M.

Library of Congress Cataloging-in-Publication Data
London, Jonathan, 1947-
Moshi moshi / by Jonathan London; illustrated by Yoshi Miyake.
p.   cm.
Summary: A young boy reluctantly accompanies his older brother
to Japan, but after spending the summer visiting his pen pal and
learning about that country's customs, he is glad that he went.
ISBN 0-7613-0110-0 (lib. bdg.)
[1. Japan—Fiction. 2. Brothers—Fiction.] I. Miyake, Yoshi, ill. II. Title.
PZ7.L8432Mo   1998
[E]—dc21   97-10612   CIP   AC

Printed in the United States of America
Published by The Millbrook Press, Inc.
2 Old New Milford Road, Brookfield, Connecticut 06804
5 4 3 2 1

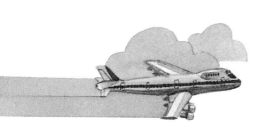

Me and my big brother Elliot—
who I sometimes call Idiot—
flew beyond an ocean of fish
to the Land of the Rising Sun,
to see Kenji, a total stranger.

We called him from the airport:
"Moshi moshi!" he said.
"Moshi moshi!" I said.
That means "hello"—on the phone.
I liked saying it: "Moshi moshi!"
But still, I wished I was home
with my friends.

It was all Kenji's idea, you see.
He had written my class.
He wanted a pen pal, and he wanted a boy
to come visit next summer, in Japan,
and become his friend.

My folks said, "What a great experience!"
Of course, *they* didn't have to go.

Kenji lived on a farm,
but he was staying with his uncle
in Tokyo, a city with a gadzillion people.

Uncle Akira drove us home
and served us tea.

He asked what I like to do.
"Ninja stuff," I said.
So he dressed me up
in a Japanese sword-fighting suit
and led me to the *dojo* on his roof—
a special room for martial arts.

Uncle Akira was a master at kendo.
He handed me a sword made of
bamboo, bowed, and came at me like
a *samurai.* Whack whack whack!
"*Mem! Doh! Koté!*"

Good thing it wasn't a real sword:
I would have been sliced into *teriyaki*—
thin strips of meat.

Elliot laughed. So did Kenji.
Some friend.

Afterward, at a restaurant,
we ate *unagi*—eel.
(Live eels squirmed in a tank by the door.)
Elliot ate his and said, "*Oishi!*"—yummy.
But I just poked at mine with my *hashi* sticks.
It still seemed to squirm.
I filled up on rice. Rice is nice.

Kenji and Uncle Akira burped happily.
So Elliot and I did, too.
Mom would have yelled at me.
Dad would have said, "Leave the room!"

That night, as we lay on *futons* on the floor,
I said, "Kenji, you said you lived on a farm!"
"I do!" he said.

In the morning we took a slow train called
the *Donko*. Uncle Akira called it "the milk run."
It stopped in every village.

Between villages, we saw farmers in wide
straw hats bent over double in the rice
paddies. As we rattled by, they stood and
waved. We waved back.

Kenji's was a Satsuma Mandarin orange farm.
I got to climb tall ladders in the trees,
and help prune the little round oranges.
Kenji's face smiled at me through the branches.

I dropped an orange on Elliot's head.
"Nerd!" he said. "Idiot!" I said.

In Kenji's house we watched TV
in a room with paper walls.
There was a war movie on,
but Kenji's mom changed the channel.
We watched baseball instead.
I love baseball more than anything—
Kenji too! Only he called it *beisu boru*.

Before dark, we ran outside to play catch.
I was starting to like him—a little.

After a week I said, "Kenji,
I'm tired of pruning oranges!"
So Uncle Akira took us and Kenji's sister
Yumiko to Kyoto, a town of temples and
gardens.

Scary monsters guarded the temple
gates. Dwarf gardeners squatted like
mushrooms in moss gardens with twisty
trees called *bonsai*. Trees so short you felt
like a giant. Moss so thick you sank to
your knees.

Then we sank to our knees, not in the moss, but in a teahouse. The tea ceremony was called *chanoyu*.
A man in a kimono whipped tea in a bowl. The tea smelled good, but it took so long to get served, my knees hurt.
I told Elliot.

He said, "Shh. Quiet. Listen to the wind in the pines."

All I heard was a motorcycle, or a chain saw.
"Idiot," I said, under my breath.
I was tired of sitting on my knees.
I darted a nasty look at Kenji.

But that night we danced barefoot on
the beach around a big bonfire
in what Kenji called an *O-bon* festival—
a festival for the dead.

We wore summer kimonos called *yukata*
and danced to drums, our arms spread
like wings. Squid hung like clothes on
lines nearby to dry.

Paper lanterns swung in the pines.
And when the drums stopped beating,
I could hear the breeze in the trees.
And the soft hush of the sea.
"Hey," I told Kenji, "this is fun!"

Back on the farm, it was almost time
to go back home. Elliot wrote a short poem
called a *haiku*, and read it out loud:

> *This is not haiku.*
> *This is high <u>key</u>, not hai<u>ku</u>.*
> *Haiku is <u>low</u> key.*

And he called it: Low Key Haiku.

I giggled, and for the first time,
I didn't think Elliot was such an idiot—
for a little while anyway.

Then I read a *haiku* of my own:

Cartwheeling like mad
around Kenji's orange farm—
Oops! Hand in cow-pie!

This time even Kenji's sister giggled.
She hid her mouth behind her hand.

Kenji beamed, and socked my arm.
I socked him back, and we laughed.
I asked him if he would be my pen pal.

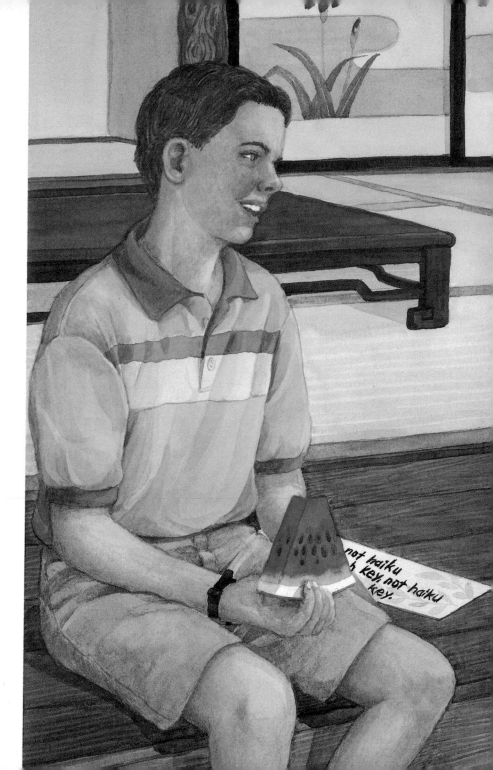

When we said goodbye, we exchanged gifts.
I gave Kenji a gold pen from America,
and said, "Be sure to write, pen pal!"

He gave me a *sumi* brush and black ink,
and said, "Be sure to write, pen pal!"

Uncle Akira gave me a plastic *katana*.
It looked like a real *samurai* sword.

We all said, "*Domo arigato gozaimasu*,"
thanking each other and bowing,
bobbing up and down. I was careful
not to bump heads.

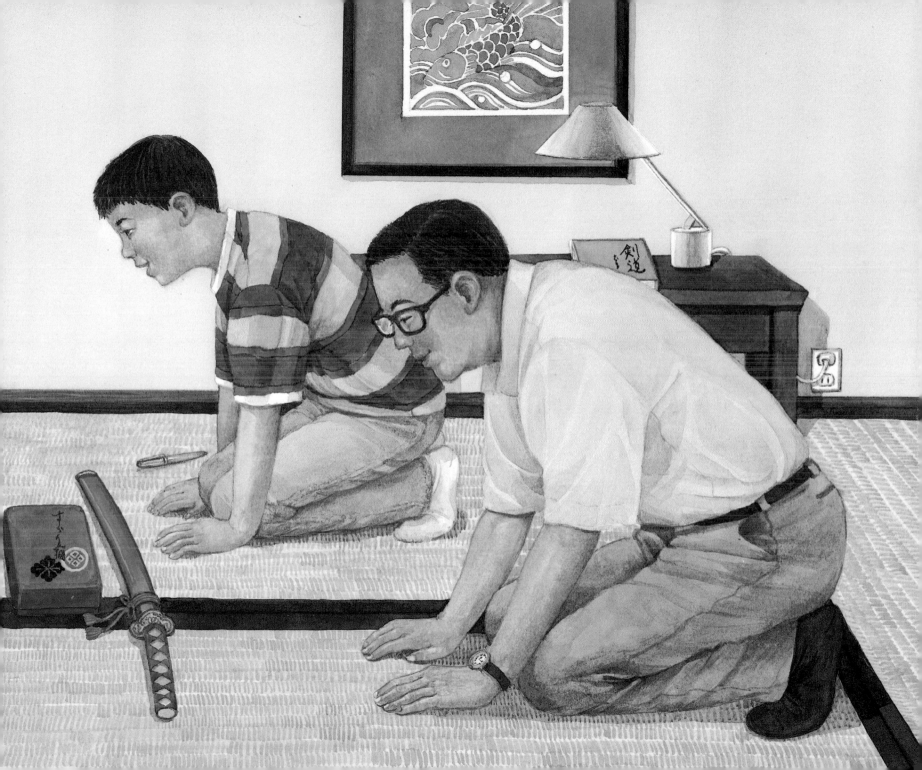

When Elliot and I got back home,
I thought about how everything in Japan
was so different from here.
Yet really the same.
It's hard to explain.
I wrote Kenji about it.
He wrote me a letter back, which said:

"The whole countries in the world hope peace."

He talks and writes English like that,
but I knew what he meant.
I was going to write him again...

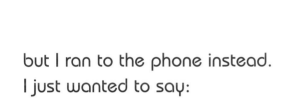

but I ran to the phone instead.
I just wanted to say:

"Moshi moshi!"